The Guinea-Pig Party

HOLLY WEBB

Illustrated by
Rosie Butcher

Barrington Stoke

Published by Barrington Stoke
An imprint of HarperCollins*Publishers*
Westerhill Road, Bishopbriggs, Glasgow, G64 2QT

www.barringtonstoke.co.uk

HarperCollins*Publishers*
Macken House, 39/40 Mayor Street Upper,
Dublin 1, DO1 C9W8, Ireland

First published in 2025

Text © 2025 Holly Webb
Illustrations © 2025 Rosie Butcher
Cover design © 2025 HarperCollins*Publishers* Limited

The moral right of Holly Webb and Rosie Butcher to be identified
as the author and illustrator of this work has been asserted in accordance
with the Copyright, Designs and Patents Act, 1988

ISBN 978-0-00-871280-8

10 9 8 7 6 5 4 3 2 1

All rights reserved. No part of this publication may be reproduced, stored in a
retrieval system, or transmitted, in whole or in any part in any form or by any
means, electronic, mechanical, photocopying, recording or otherwise without
the prior permission in writing of the publisher and copyright owners

This book is in a super-readable format for young readers
beginning their independent reading journey

A catalogue record for this book is available from the British Library

Printed and bound in India by Replika Press Pvt. Ltd.

This book contains FSC™ certified paper and other controlled
sources to ensure responsible forest management.

For more information visit: www.harpercollins.co.uk/green

*For everyone who has asked me
for a guinea-pig book!*

Contents

1 Lettuce Surprise   1

2 An Afternoon Snack   9

3 The Perfect Home   15

4 Someone New   29

5 Not Lettuce   39

6 Escape!   47

7 Katy's Plan   56

8 The Guinea-Pig Party   69

Chapter 1

Lettuce Surprise

Katy was lying on her tummy in the grass when she first saw the guinea pig.

She looked up and saw something weird in Mum's vegetable plot.

Something ginger and white in between the lettuces.

At first, Katy thought it was a bit of rubbish that had blown into the garden, but then the thing moved!

There was a noise too, a very soft munching noise, and a few little squeaks. The weird thing was eating Mum's lettuces, and it liked them a lot.

4

Katy stayed very still as the lettuce in front of the ginger-and-white animal slowly vanished and a sweet little ginger-and-white face appeared.

A guinea pig!

Katy had seen guinea pigs before at her cousin Oliver's house. He had three beautiful guinea pigs. They lived

in a big shed in his garden. Oliver had
shown her how to hold the guinea pigs,
who were all very friendly. Katy loved
cuddling them, and she loved the happy
wheezy noises they made.

She loved guinea pigs – but what
was this one doing in her mum's
vegetable plot?

"Where did you come from?" she whispered to the guinea pig. "No one in our road has guinea pigs."

Katy knew about all the different pets in their road – cats, dogs, rabbits, a tortoise. Pete, who lived two doors down, had a pet gecko called Lily. Pete fed her crickets that he kept in the freezer. Katy thought that was cool.

But no one in the street had guinea pigs.

So where had this funny little animal come from?

Chapter 2

An Afternoon Snack

Katy and the guinea pig looked at each other for a few seconds more, and then the guinea pig went back to munching lettuce. She looked as if she was hungry.

Katy thought about all the vegetables in the fridge. Would the guinea pig like something else to eat? Not just lettuce.

She knew her cousin Oliver gave his guinea pigs bits of carrot as a treat, but it was bad for them to have too many.

"Just stay there," she whispered, and she crept backwards on her tummy so as not to scare the guinea pig away. Then she jumped up and ran down the garden and in the back door.

"I'm getting some carrots sticks as a snack, Mum!" she shouted, and ran back out into the garden.

Katy ran down to the vegetable patch. Perhaps the guinea pig would be gone? But there was the vegetable patch – and there was the guinea pig!

"Hey ..." Katy said softly, and the guinea pig looked round. A long piece of lettuce was sticking out of her mouth.

"Do you like carrots?" Katy whispered, holding one out.

The guinea pig did. She scurried across the vegetable patch to Katy at top speed.

Katy sat back and watched the ginger-and-white piglet snuffle up the carrot. Then Katy fed her a handful of green grass.

Can I keep you? Katy thought. She'd always wanted a pet of her very own.

Chapter 3

The Perfect Home

Katy knew the perfect spot to keep the guinea pig.

Mum had a new greenhouse that was very smart and shiny. But the old greenhouse was still at the end of the garden.

It was a bit rusty, and some of the glass panels were missing from the roof, but it was a brilliant guinea-pig home.

No one went ever went in it – except for Katy. She had an old garden chair in there, and an upside-down plastic box for a table. It was her secret den.

Katy picked a really juicy lettuce leaf
from the vegetable patch. She held it
in front of the guinea pig's nose. "Come
on," she whispered. "Please ..."

The guinea pig's nose twitched, and
she reached for the lettuce leaf. She
squeaked loudly as if she was excited.

Katy grinned and started to walk slowly backwards with the lettuce in front of her.

"I think I'm going to call you Lettuce," she murmured. "It's your favourite thing!"

Lettuce pattered after Katy through the grass. Every so often, she came close enough to nibble a corner of lettuce, and Katy could hear her crunching it up.

"This is going to be your house," Katy said as she led Lettuce into the greenhouse. She sat down on the floor and gave her the rest of the lettuce leaf to eat.

Lettuce gobbled it all up and then sniffed at Katy's fingers.

Katy thought she was looking for something else to eat, but then the little guinea pig put her front feet up on Katy's knee and sniffed her shorts.

She was squeaking again, but she sounded happy, as if she wanted to find out more about Katy.

Then Lettuce hopped into Katy's lap and settled herself down. Katy didn't dare move. Lettuce liked her!

Very gently, Katy stroked one finger over Lettuce's smooth ginger-and-white fur. The little piglet gave another happy squeak, and Katy kept on stroking her, over and over.

Lettuce definitely liked people, and laps, and cuddling, Katy thought. Her owner must have looked after her very well. In fact, her owner must be missing her.

Katy didn't like thinking about that. She shook her head crossly. Lettuce was her pet now.

Katy looked around the old greenhouse for the things that Lettuce would need. Oliver fed his guinea pigs hay and let them out in the garden to nibble grass. Katy didn't have any hay, but the grass was easy.

A water bowl – that was easy too. There were lots of old saucers for standing flower pots in, and she could fill one up from the garden tap.

But what about the floor in the old greenhouse? Oliver had told Katy that guinea pigs had soft little feet. They needed comfy bedding on the floor of their hutches, as well as cosy hay to sleep in, or maybe a special snuggly nest. Katy didn't have any of that.

She looked at Lettuce, who was snuffling at her shorts. What could she do to make Lettuce comfy?

In Dad's home office, there was a bin full of shredded paper. It wasn't proper guinea-pig bedding, but it would do as a start.

Maybe if she told Oliver about Lettuce, he would give her the right sort of bedding? But Katy didn't want to let anyone else know her secret. She wanted to keep Lettuce all to herself.

Chapter 4

Someone New

Katy spent most of Sunday playing with Lettuce and making a big fuss of her.

Then on Monday morning, Katy nipped out into the garden while Mum was cleaning up after breakfast. She took the apple slices out of her lunch box down to the old greenhouse.

Lettuce popped out of the box of shredded paper that Katy had made her as a bed. She made lots of little wheeking noises.

She was very happy with the apple slices too. Katy only gave her two of them and some more big handfuls of grass. She didn't want to upset Lettuce's tummy.

"I've got to go to school now," Katy said as Lettuce chomped the apple. "But I'll be back this afternoon," she promised. "I'll find you some more fun things to play with."

Katy was walking slowly along the pavement thinking about what she had at home that would be a good guinea-pig toy, when Mum nudged her.

"Katy, look! The house at the end of the road – new people must have moved in over the weekend. There's a girl the same age as you. I think she's going to your school too."

Katy looked up quickly. No one else from school lived on her road.

Mum was right – there was a girl
in the blue cardigan from Katy's school
coming out of the gate with her dad.

She looked a bit nervous, Katy thought.

She waved at the new girl, and the girl smiled and waved back.

"Go and say hello," Mum said, and Katy nodded.

She walked quickly over. "Hello! I'm Katy," she said. "Have you just moved in?"

"Yes, on Friday. I'm Isabel. Are you in Year Four?" the girl asked. "I'm in Miss Ford's class."

"Me too! You could walk with us if you like?"

Isabel was a little bit shy but friendly, and it was nice for Katy to be the person who knew all about school. She told Isabel who each of the teachers were, and about lunchtimes and playtime.

When they got into class, Miss Ford let Isabel sit next to Katy. She asked if Katy could show Isabel around. *Maybe Isabel would like to come over one day after school*, Katie thought.

But then she remembered Lettuce. She couldn't let anyone meet her secret guinea pig ...

Chapter 5
Not Lettuce

After break, Miss Ford asked Isabel if she'd like to say hello and tell the class something about herself.

She did say that Isabel didn't have to if she didn't feel like it, but by then everyone was listening.

Isabel stood up in front of Miss Ford's desk.

"What do you like doing at home, Isabel?" Miss Ford suggested. "Or do you have any pets?"

Isabel smiled and nodded. "I've got two guinea pigs called Cookie and Biscuit," she said. "Cookie's got long brown fur and really dark eyes like two little chocolate chips. And Biscuit ..."

Then she stopped talking, and she looked as if she was going to cry. "I forgot," she whispered.

Katy frowned, feeling worried. Isabel looked so sad.

"What's wrong?" she whispered.

Isabel was supposed to be telling the whole class, but she looked at Katy as she began to explain.

"I don't have Biscuit any more. She was my ginger-and-white guinea pig, and she was Cookie's best friend. But she got lost at the weekend when we were moving house, and now Cookie's all on her own."

Katy felt as if her tummy had turned over inside her. A ginger-and-white guinea pig!

It had to be Lettuce.

Miss Ford said something nice about Isabel maybe finding Biscuit soon and let her sit down.

Isabel sat staring at her new reading book, and Katy didn't know what to say to her. Isabel was trying not to cry.

Isabel's house was very near Katy's, and there was a little path along the back of the gardens, next to the football field. It wasn't far for a guinea pig to go exploring.

Lettuce – or Biscuit – must have pattered along the path until she sniffed out Mum's vegetable patch, then wriggled her way under the fence.

Katy had stolen Isabel's guinea pig!

Chapter 6

Escape!

"I'm sorry about your guinea pig," Katy told Isabel as she showed her where to line up for lunch. She didn't really want to talk about Biscuit, but she had to say something. "What happened?"

Isabel sighed.

"The hutch where Cookie and Biscuit live must have got bumped in the moving lorry," she explained.

"One of the pieces of wood at the back cracked. I took them out of their travelling box and put them in the hutch at our new house – and when I went to feed them the next morning, Biscuit was gone. She squeezed through a teeny-tiny gap. Dad says she's an escapologist." Isabel sniffed.

"Oh no ..." Katy whispered.

"The worst thing is that Cookie doesn't know where Biscuit is." Isabel's voice wobbled. "Every time I go to feed her, she rushes up to the front of her hutch and squeaks at me, but she doesn't want her food. It's because she thinks I'm going to bring Biscuit back."

Isabel rubbed her eyes as if she was going to cry. "She didn't even want to eat her lettuce this morning. That's her favourite food. And Biscuit's favourite food too."

Katy swallowed hard. Now she knew that Lettuce must be Isabel's guinea pig, and her real name was Biscuit.

She knew she should tell Isabel right away that Biscuit was safe, but she just couldn't. She didn't want to give Biscuit back.

Isabel went on talking. "In the afternoon, I went out to look for Biscuit, and I took Cookie with me in her carry box," she said.

"I thought maybe Cookie would call for her, and Biscuit would hear and come back. I walked down our street, and then I went along the path at the end of the garden. But we didn't find her. I suppose she could be anywhere. I'm going to keep on trying though. Every day when I get home from school. I've got to find her."

Isabel sniffed again, and Katy put an arm around her. She felt so bad and knew she should tell Isabel that she had Biscuit.

What was she going to do? Somehow, she had to find a way to give Biscuit-Lettuce back.

Chapter 7
Katy's Plan

"I have to tell Isabel I've got you," Katy whispered to Lettuce that evening.

She knew that Biscuit was the guinea pig's real name, not Lettuce. It was hard to call her Biscuit though.

"I just don't know what to say. I really like Isabel, and I want to be friends. I need to tell her I found you. I should have told her right away. But I didn't, and now she'll hate me!

"I should have given you back before. I knew you weren't really mine. I should have told Mum and Dad so we could try to find your owners."

Biscuit snuffled at Katy's school skirt and then went to nibble the fresh grass Katy had picked for her. She was so comfy in her little greenhouse home.

Katy frowned. Maybe she could show Isabel how well she'd looked after Biscuit. Then Isabel would be happy to get Biscuit back safe and sound, and she wouldn't be cross with Katy!

It might work ...

Katy gave Biscuit the bits of carrot that she'd saved from lunch and patted her softly. Then she ran back to the house. She needed to make a plan so that Isabel would come and find Biscuit, see how happy she was and not be cross.

*

The next afternoon, Katy reached up high to tie the string of little paper flags she'd made across the old greenhouse door. The flags were in the shape of carrots and lettuce leaves – Biscuit's favourite foods.

Katy had made four paper hats too. They were sitting ready on the plastic box table, two big ones and two small ones. There was a plate of carrot sticks and lettuce and slices of apple – and a bag of sweets that Katy had saved from her birthday.

"I hope Isabel's coming," she whispered to Biscuit. "I put the invitation in her backpack – I did it when I asked Miss Ford if I could go to the loo. I hope she found it when she got her homework out."

The invitation said:

"To Isabel and Cookie.
Please come to a special
Guinea-Pig Party
at Katy's house after school.
Follow the footprints!"

Katy looked quickly at the fence at the end of the garden. There was a gate onto the path at the back, and Katy had left it just a little bit open.

She'd made some teeny piglet footprints out of paper as well and laid them all along the path between Isabel's garden and hers.

Katy had thought Isabel would be here by now. Maybe she hadn't opened her backpack and found the invitation?

Wait – was that a flash of blue school cardigan, and a face peeping round the gate?

Chapter 8

The Guinea-Pig Party

Slowly, Isabel pushed the gate open and followed the paper pawprints over the grass to the old greenhouse.

She was carrying a little plastic travel box – she had Cookie with her, just as Katy had said on her invitation.

Isabel slid open the glass door of the greenhouse and looked at the paper hats and the food. "Hello, Katy! Is it a party to cheer me and Cookie up?" she asked.

But she didn't wait for an answer. She gasped and put down Cookie's travel box with hands that shook.

"Biscuit!" she whispered, and reached out to the little ginger-and-white guinea pig, who came scurrying up to her.

She cuddled Biscuit close and then held her out, looking at her all over, trying to see if she was OK.

Then Isabel crouched down and opened up the travel box so that Biscuit could climb inside and see Cookie.

The guinea pigs made a lot of noise with excited squeaks and wheeks as they fussed over each other.

Katy watched, waiting.

"You had her?" Isabel said. "All this time?"

"I didn't know she was your guinea pig," Katy tried to explain. "I found her eating my mum's lettuces. I didn't know who she belonged to!"

"But I told you I'd lost Biscuit! I told you yesterday!"

Katy looked down at her feet.

"I know," she said. "As soon as you told me about Biscuit, I wanted to give her back. But I thought you'd be so angry with me for trying to keep her. I was scared."

Isabel looked round the greenhouse – at the shredded-paper bed and Katy's party decorations.

"You sent me a party invitation, and you laid that trail for me and Cookie," she said slowly. "You wanted us to come and find Biscuit."

"It was a way to say sorry," Katy said, and her voice went wobbly. "It's silly."

Isabel stared at her for a moment, and then she opened the travel box again. Cookie and Biscuit came slowly out with their noses twitching.

Katy picked up the plate of carrot and apple and held it out to Isabel – since they were her guinea pigs.

"You can feed them," Isabel said. "But I get to put the paper hats on, OK?"

"Yes!" Katy put the plate down in front of the two guinea pigs, and Biscuit climbed right onto it and began to eat an apple slice. Cookie climbed on too.

Isabel put a small paper hat on each guinea-pig head, and then she put the pink hat with stars on Katy and the blue one with hearts on herself.

The guinea pigs didn't seem to mind the hats at all, even though they didn't stay straight. Katy thought they looked more cute lopsided.

"I'm sorry," she said again, but Isabel gave her a teeny smile.

"You kept her safe. Anything could have happened to her. I suppose if I'd found an adorable guinea pig in my garden, I'd try to keep her too."

Katy watched Biscuit and Cookie trying to gobble the same piece of carrot. "She is adorable. They both are."

Isabel gave Biscuit a different carrot stick and then picked her up gently and sat her on Katy's lap. "Why don't you come to my house tomorrow?" she said. "We could have another guinea-pig party."

Katy smiled at her and stroked Biscuit's smooth ginger-and-white fur. "Yes, please!"

Our books are tested
for children and young people by
children and young people.

Thanks to everyone who consulted on
a manuscript for their time and effort in
helping us to make our books better
for our readers.